The Kidnapping

The Kidnapping

by Jerry B. Jenkins

cover by Lou Specker

illustrated by Richard Wahl

STANDARD PUBLISHING
Cincinnati, Ohio   2944

Library of Congress Cataloging in Publication Data

Jenkins, Jerry B.
    The kidnapping.

    (The Bradford family adventures; 4)
    Summary: While visiting a marine aquarium in Florida,
Yolanda and Daniel overhear a conversation about a plot to kid-
nap some giant sea creatures, and are soon busy carrying out a
counterplot of their own.
    [1. Mystery and detective stories. 2. Kidnapping—
Fiction. 3. Marine aquariums—Fiction] I. Wahl,
Richard, 1939-   ill. II. Title. III. Series: Jenkins,
Jerry B.   Bradford family adventures; 4.
PZ7.J4138Ki 1984   [Fic]   83-24176
ISBN 0-87239-794-7

Dedication

To Joe Ragont

Contents

In this adventure,
Daniel Bradford
tells the story.

1

The Announcement

We have a lot of smart people in our family, but none of us would have ever figured how much trouble we could get into in just three weeks.

Three weeks. That's all we had over Christmas vacation. We were going to Florida with Dad. It wasn't supposed to be anything unusual. I mean, we'd taken holiday trips before — but not to Florida.

Lots of people go to Florida in December, of course, but not for the same reason my dad does. He's Colonel Robert Bradford of the US Air Force. He's a test pilot who goes to Cape Canaveral about every other month to work at the space center.

He's not an astronaut. He says he's too old for that, but there are astronauts over forty. What he means is that he didn't get into astronaut training when he was younger, which he would have had to do if he really wanted to become an astronaut.

We had all wanted to go to Florida sometime with Dad. When your dad leaves every few weeks, and is gone for several days at a time, you sort of want to know where he is and what he's doing.

I remember the morning at breakfast when Dad announced the trip. I don't think it went over with us quite the way he expected. He said, "Well, Lillian," which is what he often says when he's about to make an announcement. Lillian's my mother, of course.

"Well, Lillian," he said, "I think this is the year we can go to Florida together."

"*This* year, Dad?" my big brother Jim asked. "You don't really mean this year, do you?"

"This year, Jim," Dad repeated. "Why not?"

"There's only three more months left in this year. You mean next summer, don't you?"

"No, I mean this year. Over Christmas break."

"Dad!" Jim and Maryann said together. Maryann's my big sister. I mean my older sister. She's not big, and she doesn't want me to call her that. In fact, she's not much bigger than I am, and I'm in sixth grade. She's a sophomore in high school.

Well, even before they told Dad what the big problem was, I knew. So did my little sister, Yo-Yo. That's not her real name. That's the nickname she picked up at the children's home before we adopted her. Her real name is Yolanda. She used to be Yolanda Treviño. Her friends put the first syllable of her first name together with the last syllable of her last name, and it came out Yo-Yo.

Yolanda is ten, and she was born in Mexico. Her skin is a beautiful light brown, and she has huge, black eyes and sparkly white teeth. We see them a lot, because she smiles so much.

Those eyes of hers were twinkling at breakfast because she knew exactly why Jim and Maryann were so shocked at Dad's idea. "We can't go in December," she said, smiling.

"Why not?" Dad asked.

"Because of basketball! All I've been hearing since I joined this family is that Jim is this great basketball star, and Maryann is a cheerleader."

Dad smacked his forehead. "Of course," he said. "What was I thinking of? You must have one of your holiday tournaments during the Christmas break."

"We do," Jim said, nodding as he swallowed a mouthful of scrambled eggs "Only we don't know where it'll be yet. Supposed to be out of state somewhere. I was hoping you could come."

"I'd like to," Dad said, "but the testing we're doing in December is important to the space shot next summer. I don't think there's any way I can get out of it."

"Well, I don't think I can get out of my tournament either, Dad, even though you know I'd love to go to Florida."

"Even if you wanted to, Jim," Mom said, "your coach would never forgive us for taking you from the team for even one game — let alone a tournament."

"Anyway, Jim," Dad said, "you have a responsibility to your team. Since NASA is paying for families to come, we may go anyway and take Daniel and Yolanda."

"NASA?" Yolanda said. "Who's NASA?"

"The National Aeronautics and Space Administration," I told her, proud of myself for remembering it all.

"I suppose the cheerleaders will get to go to wherever this holiday tournament will be," Mom suggested.

Maryann nodded, finishing her breakfast and getting up. "We'll find out this week where it is. We were kind of hoping it would be in Hawaii."

We all laughed. "Or Mexico," Yolanda squealed, and we laughed some more.

"Maybe you could take Yo-Yo to the *Gulf* of Mexico anyway, Dad," Jim said. "As long as you'll be in Florida."

"Wish I could," Dad said, "but that's all the way over on the west side of the state. I'm afraid we'll be going down the east side, through Jacksonville and St. Augustine and Daytona Beach to the Cape — and returning the same way."

"St. Augustine?" Jim said, also rising. "Isn't that where Marineland is?"

Dad nodded.

"It *is*?" I shouted. "Can we go there?"

"On the way back," Dad said. "That's part of the plan."

I hooted and hollered until Mom told me to pipe down. I noticed Yolanda had that look like she wasn't sure what I was so excited about and she couldn't wait until I told her.

"I wish I could go," Jim said. Calling upstairs to Maryann, he asked if she was riding to school with him. "I'm starting the car!" he added.

Of course, there was nothing that would stop a varsity basketball star, a senior forward who was all-state and second team all-American as a junior, from playing every game of his last year. But Marineland really was hard for Jim to pass up.

They were happy, happy, happy!

He's a swimmer and a diver. Every summer, since he was a freshman, he has worked at construction during the day and as a lifeguard at night and on weekends. He bought his Camaro and his scuba diving equipment with his own money.

There was no need for him to save money for college, or for Mom and Dad to worry about it. Jim had already been called or written to by almost a hundred college basketball coaches. He would be getting a scholarship for sure, and to just about any college or university he wanted to attend.

He had been promising to teach me how to dive, but there never seemed to be enough time.

Yolanda and I skipped nearly all the way to school that day. We were so excited. And the more I told her about all the neat places we would see in Florida, the wider her eyes grew.

That night at dinner — which was always late because of basketball and cheerleading practice — it was Jim and Maryann who had the twinkly eyes and the funny looks.

"Okay," Dad said, "what's going on with you two?"

Jim and Maryann smiled at each other. "You want to tell them?" Jim asked.

"No," Maryann said, shaking her head and

making her long, dark hair bounce. "You can."

"Well, Lillian," Jim began, just like Dad always did, "we have an announcement to make."

"We gathered that," Dad said, smiling.

"It's about the holiday tournament," Jim said.

"There isn't one," Mom guessed.

"Wrong," Jim said. "We went to the coach today and asked him when and where it was. He said he could tell us if we promised not to tell anyone else, because he's not telling the team until Friday."

"So did you promise?" Yolanda asked. "I can't imagine either of you keeping a secret until Friday."

Everyone laughed, but Jim said, "That's the problem. It's harder to keep a secret among five people than two. Can we trust you?"

Yo-Yo and Mom and I insisted that we could be trusted. Dad just sat there smiling. "Who would I tell?" he asked.

"All right," Jim said slowly. "I guess we can tell you. We're going by bus."

"That means it's close by," Mom said. "I'll bet it's in Ohio."

"Nope," Maryann said. "But we're going through Cincinnati."

Jim continued. "It's in the south."

"Louisville, Kentucky," Dad guessed.

"No, but we'll be going through there, too," Jim said.

"Nashville," Mom guessed.

"We're going through there, and Knoxville," Maryann said. "Keep going."

"You're going through both Nashville *and* Knoxville?" Dad said. "Sounds like you're zig-zagging through the South."

"We will, sort of," Jim said. "I'll give you another hint. We're also going through Chattanooga and Atlanta."

"Both?" Mom said. "My next guess was Atlanta."

"Mine, too," Dad said. "Sounds like a long, long trip."

"It is," Maryann said. "Basketball and education, the coach says. We're going to go through Americus, Georgia, too, and swing over to Plains to see where former President Jimmy Carter is from."

"That puts you pretty close to Florida," Dad said.

"Right," Jim said, "and about three hundred miles from the tournament."

Dad sat back and folded his arms across his chest. He was smiling. He had figured it out. Yo-Yo and I hadn't. We didn't know where all those cities were without looking at a map.

Jim turned to Mom and called her by her first

name again, just for fun. "While you and Dad and Daniel and Yolanda are at Cape Canaveral, Lillian, Maryann and I will be less than fifty miles to the west, in Orlando, Florida."

That was great news. Even better news was coming the next day. But the trip itself would be almost more trouble — and danger — than it was worth.

2

The
Trip
South

By the end of that week, Dad had made a deal with the basketball coach — a deal that worked out wonderfully for our family.

Dad agreed to be the personal host and tour guide for the high school team if they wanted to visit Cape Canaveral and space center during their visit to Florida. In exchange for that, the coach agreed to let Jim and Maryann make the trip with our family, rather than on the bus with the players and coaches and cheerleaders and sponsors.

The only thing Dad had to promise, besides leading a tour of the space center, was that he would take the same route as the bus. Then Jim and Maryann could see the same sights as the others on their educational trip.

Jim and Maryann weren't too sure what they thought about that at first. They really wanted to enjoy the time with their friends. But Dad reminded them that this would probably be the last time our family would be together for a trip again. He asked them to at least pray about it.

Jim was a little embarrassed that Dad had gone to the coach to make a deal without Jim knowing, but he promised to pray about it anyway. Maryann agreed immediately to go with us, even though I knew she really wanted to go on the team bus.

A couple of days later, Jim said that if it meant that much to Dad and Mom, he would go with us, too. Dad said he would let them spend time with their friends every evening, and, of course, they would be with the group for the tournament in Orlando. Next year, Jim will be traveling with some big university team, and Maryann will be gone, too, in a few years.

Yo-Yo and I thought it was too good to be true. I never thought either of them would travel with us when they could be with their friends. I didn't know what I'd do if I had to make the same choice. But, of course, Yolanda is my best friend anyway, besides being my new sister, so I probably would have chosen to go with her.

She was so new to the family that she didn't

know Jim and Maryann's bad points. They didn't have that many, but they had gotten on my nerves a lot before Yo-Yo became part of the family.

That was one of the reasons I had wanted a brother or sister my age. When they were irritable, or when they thought I was a brat or in the way, they sometimes tried to act like parents. I didn't need that. I already had my parents.

I also knew that sometime, somewhere on that long trip we would take in December, we'd all get on each other's nerves now and then, but Dad had a solution for that, too. Instead of driving us down there in the big station wagon, Dad was thinking about renting a van.

But he wound up doing better than that. He found a big recreational vehicle that was like a house trailer, only it wasn't a trailer. Instead of pulling it behind a car, you drove it just like a truck from inside.

When Dad brought it home a few days before we were supposed to leave, Mom refused to even try to drive it. I know she could have, because she was a good driver. She never had trouble with the station wagon. She even drove the neighbor's van once.

But she said she was worried about damaging it, when it didn't belong to us. Luckily, Jim had

25

just turned eighteen, so Dad spent a few hours teaching him to drive it. That way they could share the job.

The best thing about the motor home for me was that it had room enough so Jim could take his aqualung scuba equipment. I was afraid if we drove the car our luggage would take all the room. Then I'd never get Jim to teach me how to scuba dive.

As it turned out, if it hadn't been for Jim teaching me to dive, I wouldn't have gotten us into all the trouble. But I didn't know that then. If I had, I probably wouldn't have wanted to go at all.

The trip south was as much fun and excitement for Yo-Yo and me as it was for Jim and Maryann. But they had to study and take notes on all the educational places they saw in Louisville, Nashville, Knoxville, Chattanooga, Atlanta, Americus, and Plains. We just ran around and explored and listened to what we wanted and ignored what we didn't. We learned a lot just by listening to Jim and Maryann tell Mom and Dad what they had learned.

That was one of the good things about traveling with my parents. They let us go off on our own a lot. As long as we stayed within walking distance and didn't get off on side streets, we could check out anything we wanted and listen to tour guides.

The first part of the trip was so much fun. It went fast, of course, because we only had three weeks. Dad had to get to the Cape for three days of test flying before we headed back. The big trip to Marineland was to be on the way back.

I was most excited about that — and seeing Jim play in the tournament in Orlando. I had seen him play at Logan High back home, and in some other nearby schools, but I had never seen him in a big tournament, let alone one in Florida.

His team had not been good enough for the play offs the year before, even though he averaged almost thirty points a game. But this year, by the time we left for the trip, his team was undefeated and ranked among the best in the state.

Jim had started off even stronger than the year before, and he was averaging over thirty points a game, plus leading the league in rebounds. The team was rated in the top four of the Orlando tournament, which included the sixteen best teams from several states.

There would be four games, cutting the number of teams from sixteen to eight, and then from eight to four, and then from four to two, and then from two to the champion.

In most of the big cities we visited, Jim's coach arranged for the team to work out at a local high school or college. Dad let me watch a couple of times. I even got to shoot some baskets at the other end of the gym, or in one of the smaller gyms where the cheerleaders were practicing.

Yo-Yo loved to watch the cheerleaders (and sometimes I didn't mind, as long as they didn't talk to me and embarrass me). They were pretty and friendly, but mostly I liked to watch the basketball team.

The thing that was so good about the way Jim played was that he was so team-minded. I mean, just because he was the high scorer didn't mean he was a ball hog. He had a lot of assists, which means he passed the ball to the one who scored.

Most of all, of course, he *was* the best shooter, the fastest runner, and probably the best defensive player on the team. That's what made him all-conference and all-state and second team all-American. High scoring isn't enough. You have to be a great all-around player.

The other guys on Jim's team didn't resent him because of it. They might have been jealous, except he wasn't the type to brag. Because he was such a good team player and a nice guy, they elected him captain, and he really was the leader. I guess that made me prouder than all the rest.

Other guys who were great players bragged so much and were so selfish that no one liked them. Maybe they had a high scoring average, but they were never elected captains of their teams.

Jim was a good guy, and I was proud of him. He was a genuine Christian, too. Lots of kids from families like ours go to church and all that, but I wonder how many of them read their Bibles and pray without being told to — like Jim does.

Jim also liked to tell his friends about God. And he did it in a way that didn't make them angry or think he thought he was better than they were. Oh, Jim has his faults, don't get me wrong. But I wouldn't want anyone else's big brother.

After several days, we had driven hundreds and hundreds of miles south on Interstate 75. When we finally got into Florida, a couple of days before the tournament, we left Jim and Maryann and headed east on Route 10. They joined the team for the ride south, still on 75, to Orlando.

It wasn't long before we were in Jacksonville, the largest city in Florida, and one of its most important seaports. After we crossed the big St.

Johns River, I asked a man at the docks if Jacksonville had the biggest port in Florida.

"No, it don't, Sonny," he said, squinting in the sun. "That would be in Tampa. That's your biggest one, down there. That'd be over t'other side of the state. You goin' over there?"

"No, Sir. We're going to Cape Canaveral."

"Uh-huh. Used to work Tampa, years ago. You'd like it. Never worked the Cape, but my boy was stationed at Patrick down there. You know what that is?"

"No, Sir."

"Patrick Air Force Base."

"My dad's in the air force," I said. "He's a colonel."

The old man laughed. "Well, my boy never made colonel, I'll tell ya that. He flies little cargo planes now. You gettin' up to Pensacola — up to the museum?"

"I don't think so."

"Oh, make your dad take you there sometime. Big Naval Aviation Museum there — tells the whole history of flight. Right near the air station, the oldest one in the country." Dad said he wished he could take us there, but it was way up on the west side of the state near Alabama.

We just got a glimpse of Marineland in St. Augustine on the way down the east side of

Florida. I could hardly wait to get back there to see the shows and everything, but, of course, at that time I didn't know all the bad things that were waiting for us.

One of the most fun things we did before we got to Cape Canaveral was to stop at the Daytona 500 Speedway. For a small fee, we got to drive once around the track in that big motor home.

For a little more money, we could have had someone speed us around there a couple of times in a race car, but none of us were brave enough. Had I known what was waiting for us back in Marineland, I would have been glad I saved up some courage.

The next morning we would be at the space center. I was really curious about where Dad visited so often for his work. I didn't have any idea how large or small it was, or what it would look like.

All I knew was that so far the trip had been fantastic, and the best was yet to come: the space station, the basketball tournament, scuba diving, and Marineland.

At least I *thought* the best was yet to come.

3

The
Tournament

The more Yolanda and I learned about NASA, the more we wanted to know. Maryann and Jim would be touring the place with the basketball team later, so, instead of waiting to hear their questions and listening to Dad's answers, we had to think up our own questions.

"How long has this been here?" Yo-Yo asked. "It looks like it would take a hundred years to build some of this stuff."

"Well, it really started as a missile testing center in 1949," Dad said, "but NASA didn't really exist back then. It was about nine years later, when the National Aeronautics and Space Act was passed by the government, that NASA became a US agency."

"What does that mean?" I asked.

"Here," Dad said, handing me a leaflet just like the ones he would pass out to the high school group after the tournament. "This tells you all about it. If you write a report about it for school, you can use this leaflet for information."

The paper said that the purpose of NASA was to "plan, direct, and conduct all US aeronautic and space activities, except military."

"Except military?" I repeated. "But you're military, Dad? How come you're down here so much if NASA isn't supposed to have anything to do with the military?"

Dad was driving us in a jeep out to a nuclear generating station. "Oh, it doesn't mean that," he shouted over the sound of the engine and the wind whipping around our heads. "It just means that if anything here is related to war, the defense department would be in charge. I'm really here in a scientific role. Even the head of NASA is appointed by the President and the Senate from the civilian sector."

"The civilian sector?" Yo-Yo said. "What's that?"

"That means he's not in the army or the air force or anything like that."

"Oh, you mean he's a regular person," she said.

Dad laughed. "Yeah," he said, "guess you could

say he's a regular person. He's not in the service."

"I didn't know you were a scientist, Dad," I said.

"I'm not really. But they use me here for testing, not for military duty. I'm here because I work for the government, and I can fly a lot of the aircraft. There are a lot of real scientists here, though."

"I know," I said. "I heard there were lots of scientists here from other parts of the world."

"Right. In fact, one of the jobs of the head of NASA is to keep a close relationship with scientists. NASA has been one of the best ways the US has been able to cooperate with other countries."

Dad told us that he had been coming down to the space center for about twenty years, "before all these neighboring towns like Cocoa Beach, Titusville, and Melbourne got so big."

"How did they get so big?"

"Lots of industry came in — most of it related to the space program. That means jobs and jobs mean people and people mean business. When I started coming down here it was called Cape Kennedy, in honor of President Kennedy."

"The one who was shot."

"Right."

"Why'd they change the name to Canaveral?"

34

He's really good!

"Actually they changed it to Kennedy *from* Canaveral in 1963, after he was shot. He had really helped start the space race, so it was in honor of his support. Then they changed it back to Canaveral after ten years."

The next day, while Dad was working, Mom took Yo-Yo and me to the Merritt Island National Wildlife Refuge — 140,000 acres of trees and animals and reptiles and sand flies and mosquitoes and red bugs. What a place!

We learned that nearly half of all the species of trees in North America can be found in Florida. It seemed we saw every tree and flower and bush you could find anywhere. We were really tired at the end of the day, but we wouldn't admit it. It was Thursday, and the first game of the basketball tournament was that night. Everyone was all keyed up.

As long as Jim's team kept winning, they would play two more on Friday and — we hoped — the championship game on Saturday. Dad watched the Thursday night game with us, and then he checked us into a hotel so we could stay the next two days without him. He had to work, but he would try to come back on Saturday in time for the championship.

As it turned out, he missed Saturday's game, not because he didn't get back in time for the championship, but because Jim's team didn't play in it.

They won Thursday night in a massacre, whipping a local Florida team by thirty points. Jim had his highest game of the year with forty-one points. His team quickly became the favorite of the tournament. Everyone thought Logan High would win the championship.

They thought so even more the next morning when Logan won by ten and Jim scored thirty-four points, even though he rested almost all of the second half. The coach wanted to make sure the starting lineup was as fresh as possible for the game that evening. They would play a Texas school, one of the other undefeated teams.

That night they started with a huge lead at the end of the first quarter, even though Jim didn't score a basket. He missed several shots, so he started passing to his teammates even more. Luckily, a couple of the other guys were really hot, and they couldn't seem to miss.

By halftime, Logan High led by sixteen, even though Jim had just seven points. He only scored four points in the third period, when the Texans started to get closer. They were behind by only six going into the last quarter.

Not only did the Texas team tie the score early in the fourth period, but they also went ahead by eight points with just three minutes to play. They were clearly the better team, having come back from sixteen points down to being eight points up — a turnaround of twenty-four points in one half!

But it was then that Jim got hot. He scored six straight points and twelve for the period. At the end of the regular game, the score was tied. Jim scored six more points in the first overtime, but the score was tied again. He scored five more in the second overtime period, but the Texans won by one point.

What a disappointing way to lose your first game of the season! It made you want to cry, but Jim was a good sport. After a slow start, he had scored thirty-four points again, and he had done everything he could.

The coach told the guys not to let it get them down, because they had to play the next afternoon for the third place trophy. They would play the other semi-finals loser — a school from Louisiana that had also lost a close game.

The Logan players worked so hard Friday night that they looked slow and tired Saturday afternoon. But they wanted the third place trophy so much that they played well and won easily. Jim was taken out at the end of the third quarter with nineteen points to his credit. By then the victory was safe. They did not have to worry.

That night the Texas team won by more than twenty points over the team that had beaten Louisiana. Everyone agreed that even though Logan had finished third, it was certainly the second best team in the tournament.

Jim accepted the third place trophy. Then he was called back twice more, once for the sportsmanship trophy and once for the Most Valuable Player trophy. Were we ever proud of him!

Even though the team lost its first game of the year, Jim averaged thirty-two points in the four games — and he set a scoring record in the first one. The coach told the team that he thought the Texans were probably the best high school team in the country, so Logan couldn't be far behind.

"You guys could win the state championship back home," Dad told Jim Saturday night.

"We'll concentrate on the conference first," Jim said.

The next day after church the team bus brought everyone over to Cape Canaveral where Dad gave them the big tour. When they left, Jim and Maryann stayed with us. I just knew the trip home would be even more fun, because Jim and Maryann would be able to relax and not worry about the tournament anymore. They could just enjoy themselves.

Plus there was Marineland at St. Augustine, our last big stop before heading home. We made it to St. Augustine in time for church that night, but I confess I had trouble concentrating on the service.

I was thinking about all the fun I would have the next morning when Jim planned to teach me to scuba dive, and the next afternoon when we would see the water show.

I had no idea it would be more than just fun. *Much* more.

4
At
Dawn
With
Jim

Jim and I slept in the motor home while the rest of the family stayed in hotel rooms. Jim wasn't too excited about it at first. I think he wanted a nice, long comfortable bed to stretch out on after the tough tournament.

In fact, I couldn't even get him to talk that night. I was excited and wanted to stay up and chat. It wasn't often that I got a chance to talk to him, but he seemed more interested in his rest.

I couldn't get to sleep right away, partly because I was disappointed that he was already sleeping. But also I was too excited about the next morning. When I finally did fall asleep, the cool tropical air felt good and I slept soundly. So soundly that I was scared at first when Jim woke me up just before dawn.

"This is why I wanted us to get our sleep last night, Tiger," he said. "Start with your swimming stuff and get dressed." He always liked to call me by nicknames, and hardly ever the same one twice.

"Where we goin'?" I asked, my heart still pounding from having him wake me up out of a sound sleep.

"We're walking distance from the beach, Kid. C'mon, let's move."

"Will I need my flashlight?"

"Nah. Sun'll be up in a minute."

When I was fully awake, and realized that Jim was going to take me — just me — to the Atlantic Ocean with the scuba gear, I couldn't get dressed fast enough. I kept bumping my feet and knees and elbows and head on everything in the motor home as I whipped off my pajamas, jumped into my swimming trunks, threw on a shirt and jeans and sneakers, and scampered out.

"Ready, Hotshot?" Jim asked as I tumbled out, still staggering and not really ready to walk around. He handed me a bag, kept one, and hoisted the aqualung tanks over his shoulder. He was dressed pretty much the same way I was.

Being six-foot seven, he had to shorten his

steps so I could keep up with him as we headed through the parking lot to the hotel office. He scribbled a note to Dad, telling him where we'd be and when we'd be back. Then we went back out past the motor home through some spindly underbrush and about a half mile to the wide expanse of sandy beach.

Jim's big feet pushed deep into the sand and sprayed it back in my face whenever I strayed behind him. I learned to keep my distance. There was something I wanted to tell him, but I couldn't stay up with him long enough to get it out. Anyway, I was huffing and puffing so much from just trying to keep up that I quit trying to talk.

I wanted to tell him how proud I'd been of him in the basketball tournament, and not only that, how much I liked being his brother. I wanted to say that that would be true, and that I would be proud of him even if he wasn't a big star — even if he hadn't done so well, and even if he wasn't a basketball player at all.

And I wanted to tell him how happy I was that he got me up early and was taking me out to the water. I felt special, and it made me feel like he cared about me. It reminded me of the other time he got me up in the middle of the night, not even close to dawn.

It was one of those nights when you were supposed to be able to see a satellite or a comet or something if you looked in the right direction. He even showed me how to hang onto my belt buckle while pulling up my pants so it wouldn't make noise and wake up everyone else.

We had tiptoed downstairs and out into the yard. We were there probably forty minutes before Jim decided that it was too overcast to see anything. I didn't know how he could tell in the darkness, but he said it had something to do with how hazy the stars looked.

We didn't see anything at all, but the feeling I got from just being out there with him, and having him ask me out there in the first place, made me feel all warm. I remember I went back to bed and lay there with my eyes open for a long time, feeling lucky and special.

When I finally fell asleep again, I slept right through Saturday morning breakfast. When I came down the stairs, Mom and Dad and Maryann all asked me about Jim's and my failed mission. It made me feel good again to know that he had told everyone about it.

I wanted to tell Jim all that this morning in Florida, but he wasn't interested in talking yet. He had his eyes set on a huge outcropping of rock, dead ahead of us. "That'll be perfect," he

44

said. I couldn't imagine how we could drop into the water with the aqualung from a ten-foot-high rock that far from the water.

When we reached the rock, Jim handed me the aqualung and told me to put my bag down. He slung the other bag he had been carrying up on the rock and climbed up the back side with his long reach and strides.

"Hand me the bag first," he said, lying on his stomach and leaning over in the pale light of dawn. I could hardly see him. "Hurry," he added kindly, "so we don't miss the sunrise."

I grabbed the bag and tried to sling it up to him the way he had slung the other. Instead of landing softly in his arms or even on the rock the way his had, mine opened upside down. The aqualung hoses, Jim's flippers, and his knife fell on my head and shouders.

Luckily the knife was still in its sheath, so I didn't get hurt. The best thing was that Jim didn't laugh at me, even though I did. "That's all right," he said, explaining from his perch how to hold the bag and sling it up to him.

Then he told me how to get under the aqualung and bend my knees, hoisting it high above my head until he could reach it and pull it up. He put it down carefully next to him and reached for me. He slid up onto one knee and planted the other foot firmly. He pulled me up by the wrists as I tried to step in the right places.

Just as I settled in next to him on the rock, the middle part of the huge, orange sun peeked over the horizon. The sky exploded into all sorts of colors, and we just sat there staring at that big ball. It seemed to grow wider and flatter as it rose in the sky.

I turned away for just a second when I heard Jim digging into one of the bags. I noticed he was doing it without looking away from the sunrise, so I turned back to the horizon.

As the sun seemed to deflate a little and turn more yellowish, I realized that all I could see was sun and clouds and sky and sea. It was the most beautiful thing I had ever seen.

"Hungry?" Jim asked, handing me a yellow apple and a paring knife. He cut thick slices from a cake of cheddar cheese with his long, sharp diving knife. I'd never had a breakfast quite like it before, but it was great.

When we finished eating, Jim cleaned the knives by laying them inside the back of his knees — blade out, of course — and bending his legs to tighten his jeans around them. Then he pulled them out, clean and dry.

As the beach became a little brighter, I found myself sitting just like he did, feet flat on the

The sky exploded into all sorts of colors!

rock and pulled up close to my seat, arms around my legs, and hands locked at the knees. "Let me show you something I like to do when I get the chance," he said, reaching in his bag again.

He pulled out two Bibles, a black one and a green one, and handed me the green one. "Turn to Psalm 103 first, Dan," he said. "I'll read a few verses, and then I want you to read the same ones from your Bible. I'll start with the first two verses:

" 'Bless the Lord, O my soul: and all that is within me, bless his holy name.

" 'Bless the Lord, O my soul, and forget not all his benefits.' "

He looked up. "Now me?" I said, my voice weak. He nodded. I read: "I bless the holy name of God with all my heart. Yes, I will bless the Lord and not forget the glorious things he does for me."

"Now the eighth verse," Jim said. "The Lord is merciful and gracious, slow to anger, and plenteous in mercy." He looked up at me.

I read, "He is merciful and tender toward those who don't deserve it; he is slow to get angry and full of kindness and love."

"Now Psalm 104," Jim said. "Read verses twenty-five to twenty-eight and thirty-three,

48

okay?" I nodded. "You read it," he again repeated.

I read: "There before me lies the mighty ocean, teeming with life of every kind, both great and small. And look! See the ships! And over there, the whale you made to play in the sea. Every one of these depends on you to give them daily food. You supply it, and they gather it. You open wide your hand to feed them and they are satisfied with all your bountiful provision . . .

"I will sing to the Lord as long as I live. I will praise God to my last breath! May he be pleased by all these thoughts about him, for he is the source of all my joy."

"I feel like praying, Dan," Jim said, clapping me on the knee. "Do you?"

I did, but not out loud. I shook my head.

"Then I will," he said.

It was already the most special morning I'd ever had. And it had just begun.

5
Growing up—
All
at
Once

When Jim was finished praying, without another word he stood and moved to the front end of the huge rock. Then he jumped ten feet down to the sand. "Aqualung first," he said, reaching up with both hands.

I scrambled to get it, and I tried to keep from dragging it across the surface of the rock. Holding it by the straps, I lowered it to him, not letting the tanks bang against the side of the rock.

I shoved the Bibles back into one bag and tossed both bags down to him. He left one for me, picked up the aqualung tanks and the other bag, and strode off across the beach toward the water.

I had hoped he would help me down, but it was clear he expected me to get down myself.

He had just jumped into the sand, but of course his whole life was jumping up and down on hardwood floors. The sand was like a cushion for him.

It looked a long way down to me. I tried to climb down, but the bag kept getting in my way. I let it fall to the sand. It hit hard, just like I would if I jumped. Should I call him back to help? No, that would make me seem like a baby.

If Jim Bradford could jump down ten feet into the sand, then so could Daniel Bradford, I decided. I crept toward the edge and peered over. Oh, boy. I looked again for a way to crawl down. The first step would have been about half way down. I could never reach it.

I turned around and let my legs dangle over the side, holding tight at the top. If I pushed off, I'd have to get myself far enough away from the face of the rock so I wouldn't scrape myself as I fell.

I turned and looked down over my shoulder. My feet would have to drop only about six or seven feet. I craned my neck and saw that Jim was about forty feet away, but he was not looking back. I figured he was ignoring me on purpose.

He wanted me to get down by myself, and he wasn't going to embarrass me by watching. I pressed my toes against the rock and pushed away, but I couldn't get up the courage to let go. My body swung back, and my knees crunched into the rock.

It didn't hurt, but I knew I had to get down quickly before I made a fool of myself. How long could Jim keep ignoring me?

I pushed away again and forced myself to let go with my hands. I closed my eyes and clenched my teeth, waiting — it seemed like forever — for my feet to hit. I hoped they'd hit the sand first. If they hit the side of the rock, I'd probably wind up on my head and break my neck.

For what seemed like a whole minute, I worried that just that would happen. I'd lie there with a broken neck, and Jim would feel bad because he had only tried to let me grow up a little by getting down myself. My family would visit me in the hospital, and I would sit in a wheelchair the rest of my life.

It's amazing what can go through your mind in a split second.

And then I hit. My sneakers plunged four inches into the sand, which was soft at first and then seemed like cement. The impact made my knees buckle, and my seat slam down behind my heels.

My knees were driven into my chest. I rolled backwards with just enough speed to almost stand on my head. My feet kept going and dragged me slowly over onto my face, grinding the sand into the back of my neck, down under my collar, and then into my forehead and cheeks.

Nothing was broken. Nothing was even hurting, except for the stinging on my face. I quickly lurched to my knees and brushed everything off, grabbed the bag, and stumbled after Jim.

He was almost to the water's edge by now and was peeling down to his swimming trunks. "All set?" he asked, as I jogged up — as if I'd been right behind him all the time. I decided he was really a special brother.

When he had just his trunks on, he sat on the smooth, wet sand at the water's edge and put on his flippers. "These are going to be way too big for you," he said, "but we'll try to adjust them anyway. We won't be going that deep, but you should get used to wearing them when you're underwater with the tanks."

With the long, floppy, rubber flippers on, Jim stood and took a couple of giant steps to his bag and removed a weighted belt. "These are really hard to walk in," he said, "because they're not made for walking, anymore than a fish's tail is made for walking. You have to high step like this, or you wind up on your face."

I wondered if he could still see a few grains of sand on mine. I changed the subject . "What's the belt for?"

"Weight. We probably won't need it in this shallow water, but it helps keep you down there when you have enough air and want to stay."

"How long can you stay under?"

"With these tanks, you mean?"

"Yeah."

"These are good for about an hour. Without the tanks, I can't stay under more than about a minute and a half. Maybe two minutes — but that's pushing it."

"Two minutes! Really? That sounds like a long time to hold your breath."

"You have to be in shape, Dan. I would only be able to do that once in one day, and it would probably have to be the first or second time I went down. I've been with some experienced divers who have stayed down eight or nine minutes. But they can't go deeper than about thirty-five feet."

"You're kidding! How do they do it?"

"They work up to it. They do it every day and train themselves. One guy stayed down almost ten minutes, and we started to panic. We put on tanks and went down looking for him. He gave us the okay sign, so we let him stay down. Later, he came up huffing and puffing and pretty red —but it was impressive."

"No thanks," I said, in case Jim was about to suggest I go down without the tank.

"Me either," he said, smiling and strapping on the aqualung. The air hoses dangled around his neck as he hitched on his knife and put on what looked like a huge watch. "Depth gauge," he said, showing me the face. "I don't really need it today because we won't be going deeper than ten feet, but I feel strange without all my gear when I go down."

"What's the knife for?"

"Lots of stuff. I probably wouldn't need it today either, but I hate to go down without it. I feel safer with it in case I'm down with a line or something. If I get tangled up, I can easily cut myself free. See how sharp it is — even after cutting cheese this morning?"

He slid it out and ran his thumb lightly across the blade, slicing through the first layer of his fingerprint without drawing blood.

"Wow!" I said.

"It's also good for spearing small fish if they happen to swim close. I can open oysters or clams with it, and clean fish, too."

"Where's your spear?"

"Didn't bring it. I'll feel a little funny without it, but there would be no use for it today. It's too dangerous. Remember when I ran it through my foot?"

"Sort of. I was pretty young then."

"Yeah. It was about six years ago, just after I had gotten really interested in basketball. I was afraid I'd never play again."

"How'd you do it?"

"I was trying to spear a big, juicy frog in Woods Lake. I shot at him once and missed. Then I reloaded and went after him again. By then he was darting all over the place to get away. When he went under and behind me, I thrashed around to face him and the spear went off. I'll never forget seeing those three sharp points sticking out through the bottom of my foot. Broke two small bones and had a lot of stitches — but I was walking again within six weeks."

"What makes the spear shoot out?"

"Mine is powered by rubber springs, but professionals use metal springs or gun powder or even compressed gas. If I'd had anything like that, it probably would have taken my toes right off."

Jim spit in the waterproof face mask and

rubbed it over the glass. Then he pulled it over his head, and down over his eyes and nose. It made him sound funny when he talked. "You know why I rub the saliva around on the inside of the glass, right?"

I nodded. "To keep it from fogging up."

He nodded and fished around in his bag. He came up with a plastic snorkel unit. He motioned that I should follow as he padded toward the water.

"What's that for?" I asked.

He held up a finger and kept going, as if I should wait and see.

I had been standing on the beach with my arms folded, trying to keep warm in the morning breezes. I hadn't been doing well. My arms were covered with goose bumps, and I wished I'd kept my shirt on.

The sun was getting higher, but it was still early, and I couldn't feel much of its warmth. All I could hear were the gulls crying and the waves lapping. There was nothing else and no one around.

"Ah!" Jim shouted as the icy ocean water came over his flippers and hit his ankles. "Love it!"

"You do?" I shouted.

"No, but I always tell myself I do! You know

the secret to getting used to this water, don't you?"

"Yeah," I said, knowing he meant that I should just plunge under and get it over with. "But I'm not ready!"

I just kept edging out deeper and deeper as the water crept up, inch by inch, to my knees, my thighs, my waist. Oooh, it was cold! I kept my hands above the surface, but I knew I would have to go under sooner or later.

I remembered the time in Lake Michigan when my dad had let me slowly get out that deep. Then when he couldn't talk me into just going under, he splashed me. I hoped Jim wouldn't do that.

When he turned to say something to me, I ducked, and he laughed. "I won't splash you, Kid. I can't go under all at once either with all this gear. Besides, I want you to be able to watch what I do. Just keep coming."

Finally we were deep enough that the water was up to just under my arms. I was shivering, and I'm sure my lips were blue. My teeth were chattering, and I tried to talk to keep them from making too much noise.

"What do professional divers dive for?"

"The first ones were military," Jim said, his voice still sounding nasal because of the mask.

"Now they dive to do spear fishing, exploration, photography, commercial pearl diving, treasure hunting, that type of stuff."

"People really hunt for sunken treasure?"

"Oh, sure. There are a lot of old ships down there. If you can find them, there should be something of value, even if it isn't a chest full of gold."

6

Scuba Diving

"Just about another ten feet here, and it will be deep enough for you to stand with only your head above water," Jim said. "Ready?"

I nodded and kept walking, still trying to keep my arms above the surface. Finally he stopped. "There's a little drop-off here," he said. "Just come on by me and let your feet sink to the bottom for a second. That'll put you under, and you'll be sensitized to the water. Okay?"

I nodded, still shivering and not really ready, but I was finished being a baby about it. I slid past him. With his height, the water wasn't far above his waist. I wondered if I'd ever be that tall. It wouldn't make that much difference. I would probably never have his skill on the basketball court, and unless I had another fifty

Watch out for the drop off!

pounds, that much height wouldn't do me any good anywhere else.

My last plunge into the icy water almost made me scream, but I just bobbed back up and moved a few feet closer to the shore. Now I could stand with my head above the surface again.

"You know how to use the snorkel, right?" Jim asked. I nodded and inserted the mouthpiece, blowing and sucking to make sure the other end — the one with the valve opening — was working.

"Good," he said. "When I go under, just stretch yourself out on the surface and keep yourself on your stomach by kicking and paddling. But don't stir up the water any more than necessary. Okay?"

I nodded.

"Now turn the valve on my tank two full turns — till the arrow comes up to the top twice," he said. "Then watch me. Normally I would fall backward into the water from a pier or a boat, but out here I'll just lift my legs and let my weight take me under."

"I have a question," I said.

"Hurry," he said, as the air escaped from the hoses. "I'm wasting oxygen."

"I was just wondering why you need a weight

belt when you've got the heavy aqualung tanks."

"It isn't that heavy," he said. "And when I get in the water, the buoyancy makes it feel even lighter."

He started to go under.

"Why do you usually fall backward?" I asked quickly.

"Because if I went in head first the impact would rip my mask off and the hoses from my mouth. And the tanks would be on top of me instead of behind me. Now I gotta go under."

He inserted the mouthpiece and dropped from my sight. I pulled on my face mask and flattened out on my stomach and kicked and paddled. I had to stay close enough to the surface so my snorkel tube would allow me to breathe.

In the murky water, I could see Jim moving about in his gear. He edged out into deeper water and kicked his fins until his feet were near the surface. He was heading straight down. Then he brought his feet around under him again and stayed near the bottom.

From my position, I could see him looking at rocks and shells on the bottom. He looked up at me and pointed to his left. I looked as far as I could see underwater, but I had no idea what he was pointing at. I shrugged. He surfaced.

"There's a long coral ridge over there," he said. "We've got to get you used to this tank so we can go check it out. It'll be one of the most fantastic experiences you've ever had. Really, Daniel, there's nothing like it — especially at this time of the morning with the sun where it is and everything."

"What's that got to do with it?"

"You'll see. Here, let me help you into this gear."

We moved closer to shore. I was glad I was finally used to the water temperature. It felt better to be under the surface than sticking out where the breeze made you freeze. When we were in far enough, so that the water came to just below my waist, Jim steadied me while I put on the flippers.

They were way too big, but he tightened them behind my ankles. They felt strange and bulky, but did they ever work great! "Just paddle around with them a minute and see how they work," he said.

I stretched out in the water and kicked a big spray onto him. He ducked. I laughed and kept going. It was almost unbelievable. Every thrust of my legs made the big, rubber fins force the water behind me, and I felt myself propelled at about twice my normal speed.

I felt bigger, faster, more powerful. I tried twisting and turning in the water, the way Jim had, and the flippers made it easy. When I turned downward and kicked, I had to put my hands in front of me to keep from smacking my head on the bottom.

Even if I never learned to use the scuba equipment, this was good enough! I never wanted to swim without fins again. It was so much more fun.

Jim strapped the weighted belt around me, and then he helped me strap on the aqualung. He brought the hoses down over my head and washed off the mouthpiece. "Bite on these two little rubber pieces," he said. "And breathe normally. Get used to them before you go under."

I started sucking and blowing the same way I had with the snorkel, but Jim was waving and shaking his head. He helped me remove the mouthpiece.

"No, no," he said. "That's the most common mistake made by beginners, I did the same thing when I was learning. See this regulator? It lets you breathe normally. You don't have to work at it, like you do when you're trying to draw air through the snorkel. That's why snorkels are usually not longer than about fifteen inches.

Because it's so hard to draw air from the surface from much farther than that."

"So I'm not supposed to breathe, or what?" I asked.

"No, you breathe, but just normally. See, one of your hoses is for intake, and the other is for exhaling. The regulator can sense when you've taken in enough oxygen. Then it switches off for a second and lets you exhale — then it reverses and lets you inhale again. Try it and pretend like you're letting the tank breathe for you."

He was right. I just breathed in and out slowly, and I could feel the clicking as the regulator kicked on and off. "If you need more air, you'll naturally inhale a little harder and the regulator will give you more. Now breathe normally again and drop beneath the surface."

I lifted my feet and settled at the shallow bottom. For the first time in my life, I was breathing normally while totally underwater. When I felt myself starting to pant or breathe harder, mostly because of my fear that I would run out of oxygen or that something would go wrong with the tank, I just told myself to relax and enjoy it.

Just above me, Jim was face down with the snorkel, watching me and smiling. At least it looked like he was smiling from what I could see between his face mask and the snorkel mouthpiece. I panicked a little when he started swimming across the surface above me, leading me away.

He motioned for me to follow, and he slowed down so I could get in position. There was really nothing to be afraid of. We were in such shallow water that any time I wanted to, I could just stand up.

I put my hands out in front of me, as if to do a push-up on the bottom, and kicked my fins. Within seconds, I had passed Jim. He signaled me to keep going. He stayed nearby as I got used to skimming along underwater, breathing from the tank and moving easily with the flippers.

We swam this way for about ten minutes, until we came upon a long ridge of coral formations. I could hardly wait to get there. They looked so beautiful, like rocks painted with dozens of brilliant colors.

I gave one last flip of my fins to come within touching distance, but I was stopped almost dead in the water by Jim's strong right hand around my wrist. His yank almost made the tanks slip from my back. I looked up at him sharply.

With his right hand, he pointed to the fingers of his left hand, then at the coral, and shook his head, waving his hand back and forth. Apparently, I was not to touch the coral. I shrugged to ask why.

He pointed at my fins and motioned for me to hand him one. I struggled to slip it off. He held it carefully in front of him and slowly moved closer to the coral reef. He dragged the webbed end of the flipper very lightly over the top edge of the beautiful coral. Then he showed me the fin.

It had been sliced long and deep, as if he had slashed it with a razor-sharp knife. My eyes grew large, thinking what that blade-like rock would have done to my fingers. We both edged closer to the coral and studied it.

I was scared to death to get too close — afraid that the movement of the water might push me into it. When we surfaced, Jim told me that many divers had been injured or even killed by coral. "Some have had their air hoses slit by it before they knew what was wrong. They swallow water and have to work hard to get to the surface before they drown."

"Why did you cut your fin, just to show me how dangerous it was?"

"That won't hurt the fin, unless it went all the way through. I just had to show you how tough and sharp that coral was."

"It worked. I'm scared of it."

"That's the best way to be."

"What is that coral anyway — just rock that's been sharpened by the movement of the water?"

"Not really. The movement of the water helps sharpen it, yes. But it's not made of rock at all. Believe it or not, coral is made from the skeletons of dead sea animals. The live ones live in the holes and crevices. As they die off, and their skeletal bones are exposed, they stick together and grow sharp. You can see how sharp."

"I sure can."

7

The
Water
Show

By mid-morning, when we were retracing our steps through the underbrush and into the parking lot, I was so full of the sights and sounds and feelings of the day that I could have gone to bed right then.

The visit to Marineland was still coming up, and I wouldn't miss that for the world, but I'd already had enough good things happen to last a month.

Jim and I packed up the gear and laid in the sun until our trunks were dry. Then we gathered up everything and lugged it back to the motor home, where we found a note from Dad.

"We're in the restaurant for brunch," it read. "Join us if you're back in time."

We stowed the stuff and strolled through the

lobby of the hotel to the restaurant. The apples and cheese had filled me up. I just sat and watched Dad and Mom and Maryann and Yo-Yo eat all the fruit and eggs and cereal and rolls they wanted from the big buffet.

Jim was always hungry. A little fruit and cheese had just got his appetite going. He wound up eating more than anyone. There was a lot of pleasant talk and everything, and Mom wanted to know how the scuba diving had gone.

Jim didn't tell her everything about the morning, like the Bible reading and praying and the sunrise. I was glad he didn't. I didn't say anything about it either. It would have spoiled it — made it less special.

Maybe someday I would tell Yo-Yo or Mom or Dad, but maybe not, too. It was something Jim and I had done together, just the two of us. No talk about it could make it sound as fantastic as it was.

As long as I live, I don't think I'll ever forget the way that orange sun looked, working its way up over the water's edge at the horizon. Or how it felt to have Jim hand me that green Bible, the one I could understand so much better than the one he read from.

And I don't ever want to forget the sound in his voice when he read those verses about praising

God for all that He made and all that He does for us. I wish I had prayed when he asked me to, but I was still embarrassed to pray in front of my big brother.

It was embarrassing enough to read the Bible out loud in front of him, but somehow he made me feel all right about it, even though my voice was nervous.

Then he was so patient in teaching me to dive, explaining the aqualung and all that. He protected me from the coral, but he showed me how I could watch it and study it and see the sun dance off it. Just enjoy its beauty. Jim knew I would love how pretty it was, even though that's not something I would talk about.

Yolanda was trying to tell me how she and Mom had put their swimsuits on under their outfits. They had hoped to swim in the hotel pool before breakfast, but it was closed until late afternoon. I found it hard to listen and concentrate.

I just sat there while everyone was eating, thinking how delicious it was that I had my own secrets, my own memories of a special morning. It hurt me to think that Jim and I had spent so little time together like that before.

But I hadn't always looked up to him either. When we were younger, he didn't know as much about what I wanted or needed, and he probably didn't care. I was just in the way — a nuisance. Now that he didn't mind me being around, time was running out. He would be going off to college, and I would miss him.

That morning and those memories might have to last a long time. That was all right. They would.

There was so much to see at Marineland that afternoon that Dad let us all split up. We could go and see what we wanted, as long as we met back together every hour or so. I wanted to stick by Jim, but he and Maryann decided they wanted to see every exhibit, every animal, every show, so they got way ahead of us.

At first that bothered me, because I sort of felt that the morning had entitled me to Jim and his time for the rest of the day. But then I wondered how that would make Yolanda feel. I mean, who did I think I was that I could spend time with my big brother and leave her with nobody?

She was closer to my age. I had wanted a new brother or sister just because I didn't get enough time with my older brother and sister. Now that I *did* get some time, wasn't I going to need Yo-Yo anymore?

That was ridiculous, and I felt ashamed. I decided that I wanted to be to Yo-Yo what Jim had been to me. I didn't know how to start, or what to say or do, so I just got happy about having lots of time with her. Long after Jim and Maryann were gone off to college, Yolanda and I would be playing and talking and enjoying things together.

I knew I should tell her that. "Yo-Yo," I said, "I'm glad you're part of our family."

She stopped walking and stared at me, wondering what was wrong. I kept walking, embarrassed. "Daniel," she said, hands on her hips. I stopped and turned around. I wouldn't look into her eyes. "That was a nice thing to say," she added. "That made me feel good."

I knew she was smiling at me with those beautiful teeth of hers, so I peeked up at her. I was right. She was beaming. Now I was really embarrassed. I mean, I was glad I had told her, but what was I supposed to do now?

She started walking fast again, the way she always does when there's a lot to see and do. But as she went past me, she reached out and grabbed my hand, pulling me along with her.

The last thing in the world I wanted to do was to be seen walking around Marineland holding hands with a girl. But I had just told her how glad I was that she was my sister, so she probably felt she had a right to hold my hand.

I was dying, feeling like everyone was looking. But then I thought of how Jim did all those things with me and for me that morning. Maybe he hadn't really wanted to do that either, but he had done it anyway.

If holding Yolanda's hand would make her believe what I told her, then I guessed it was all right. As long as my hand didn't get too sweaty, or there weren't too many boys of my age around.

After a while I didn't mind holding her hand while we walked, mostly because I realized that no one was watching or seemed to care if they did. We went down into a whole bunch of underground hallways where you could see the big fish at their level.

We saw sharks and baby whales and seals and sea lions and all kinds of smaller fish, too. We kept seeing signs that said at 1:30 there was a dolphin and porpoise show. "That looks like fun," Yo-Yo said. "Let's find it."

It was already after 1:20, so we ran all over the place, following the signs and asking people. Finally we reached a big outdoor theater, set up in front of a gigantic pool of water. Hundreds of people were crowding in, laughing and talking.

We wound up sitting about ten rows from the front, behind a young black man and his

Look at that!

girlfriend or wife. We couldn't tell which. Yolanda immediately started talking to them.

"You married?" Yolanda asked.

Yo-Yo her diamond. "Are *you*?"

Yolanda giggled and introduced herself — then me.

"Well, hi," the man said, turning around and shaking hands with us. He was very light brown with short hair and cool, white shirt and pants and white socks and shoes. He wore a thin, gold chain around his neck. He said his name was Neil and his girlfriend's name was Sasha. She wore a short, green sun outfit. She was very black — and very pretty.

"What's the notebook for, Neil?" Yolanda asked. "You a reporter or something?"

"No," he said, chuckling. "I'm a student. I'm studying marine biology at Bethune-Cookman College."

"You, too, Sasha?" Yolanda said, as only she could.

"No, I'm from here in St. Augustine. Neil visits when he can, but usually when he wants to study something here."

Yolanda told her all about where we were from, why we were in Florida, and that our brother was a basketball star, the whose story. I got the feeling they thought Yo-Yo was cute, but that they were only pretending to be interested in all her talking.

"Oh, good," Yo-Yo said finally. "You'll be able to tell us what this is all about."

"I'm not so sure about that," Neil said, grinning at her. "But you can ask me whatever you want."

"You gonna take notes about this show?"

"No. I know about these animals. I've been taking notes at some of the other exhibits."

The show started. A muscular, young, blond man with lots of hair and a red face introduced the various dolphins and porpoises who leaped from the water and jumped through hoops and splashed the crowd.

One jumped up and took a cigarette from the man's mouth. There was lots of cheering and clapping and laughing. But the trainer kept promising that the best part was yet to come. That a special guest was already in the water.

"He came in through our subterranean waterways, and he has been lurking at the bottom of our pool for the last few minutes." A few girls screamed, but the trainer continued. "Oh, there's nothing to fear. It's not a shark or a monster. It's a beautiful *D. sinensis* from the China Sea!"

Neil flinched and stared at Sasha. She raised her eyebrows, as if to ask him what was so special about it. "Wait and see," he said. "You won't believe it. It's one of the most beautiful sea creatures in the world."

"I can't even tell the difference between the dolphins and the porpoises," Yolanda admitted.

"That's easy," Neil said, turning around. "The dolphins have those beak-like mouths. The porpoises have round head and no beaks. See?"

Yo-Yo nodded. "Are they related, like cousins or something?"

"Sort of. They're just slightly different species."

"Species?"

"Types. The porpoises are found in the Atlantic and the Pacific and Arctic waters. They probably got these right off the coast of Florida. Most of them aren't even eight feet long. They're the ones that are bluish black on top and whitish underneath."

"Yeah, like those," Yolanda said, pointing.

"Right," Neil said. "And those gray ones, the ones about ten feet long with the triangular tail fins are dolphins. They're found in all seas, and even some rivers. Both dolphins and porpoises have lots of small, sharp teeth. They feed on fish like salmon and mackerel and herring."

"Their skin looks so smooth," Yo-Yo said.

"It is. And you know, we think they can talk to each other. They make clicks and cries and whistles, some with their mouths and some through the blowhole in the top of their heads. They use the sounds to tell how far away things are, just like sonar or radar, and they also seem to talk with each other."

The trainer was talking again. "Another special guest has joined us at the bottom of the pool. We'll call her *D. seronii*. Her boyfriend can't stay down there much longer, because these are mammals, you know. They need to breathe eventually. So let's get everyone else out of the pool, then we'll have our special guests surface to your big welcome."

Neil shook his head as the other creatures dove to leave the pool through the waterways. "I can't believe it," he told Sasha. "One from China and one from the South seas. Wait till you see them. I had no idea they had them here."

8

The
Plot

We didn't have long to wait. Just before the two "special guests" appeared, I heard voices behind me, talking about them. One came from a distinguished-looking, older man in a light gray suit. He had short, white hair, and he wore a gold bracelet and a thick, gold ring.

The man next to him was short and stocky and muscular. He reminded me of the trainer and host of the show, except that he had dark hair and had a hoarse, raspy voice. He had to talk loud so his friend could hear him.

What he said shocked me.

"These are the ones," he said. "Wait till you see 'em."

The older man said something soft that I couldn't hear.

"Trust me," the younger man said. "I can get 'em, and they'll make you a quick profit."

Yolanda was talking to Neil and Sasha. I had to strain and find a reason to lean back so I could hear better without the men knowing. Luckily, I looked young and was sitting with a tiny girl who looked even younger. I don't think they would have worried about me, even if they knew I could hear them.

"Best way to do it is in broad daylight, Jonas," the younger man said. "Just be sure Andy has the rig near the south inlet before three o'clock."

"Where's your suit, Gary?" Jonas asked.

"Don't worry about me and my suit. I got it stashed. I'll do my part. You do yours."

"I still don't understand how you're going to get into the waterways."

"I used to work here, man. Now, don't worry about it. I got a lot more to lose than you. You can get fifty grand a piece for these beauties from a lot of different places. Just get Andy in position, and I'll see you on the boat."

"He knows how to open the hatch?"

"Yeah, yeah. Now get goin'! South inlet."

As Jonas, the older man, stood and moved toward the aisle, a great roar went up from the crowd. Two pure white dolphins, a male and a female, dove up and out of the water at the same time. They passed each other in mid-air, at least eighteen feet from the surface. When they slid into the water again, there was hardly a splash. No one could take their eyes off them.

"Are they beautiful?" the trainer called out, and the crowd clapped and screamed. "*D. sinensis* from the China Sea, and *D. seronii* from the South seas — the only trained pair of pure white dolphins in captivity!"

They swam to the opposite ends of the pool and raced back toward each other, diving and then throwing themselves high out of the water, not crossing, but spinning together as they headed back down.

"The male has been measured leaping more than twenty-one feet from the water," called the trainer. "It's all because of those powerful tail-fin muscles! And you can see his girlfriend isn't far behind!"

Neil's eyes were glued to the show as the white dolphins performed many tricks. I asked him how they got the creatures into the park, and without looking away from the show, he said, "There's an inlet to the south of here where the waterways begin. The ones that are too large for tanks are delivered there from cages on ships."

"Can we see it?"

"Oh, they're beautiful!"

"There's nothing to see unless you're under water."

"Can you get to the inlet from inside the park?"

"Only underwater," he said.

"What did you say these dolphins like to eat?"

"Salmon, herring, mackerel — and I suppose some smaller things like mollusks."

The trainer was telling the story of how these beautiful white dolphins were found and caught and transported to the United States on a special expedition. He said they were the most valuable sea creatures in the United States.

"Yolanda," I said urgently in my most serious, grown-up voice.

She turned and looked at me, but only for a second. "I want to see this," she said.

I squeezed her arm, and she pulled away. "Yo-Yo," I insisted, "we have to meet Mom and Dad soon. Let's go."

"Oh, Daniel," she whined, still watching the dolphins, "can't you just tell them I'm in here?"

"No!" I shouted, as I dragged her toward the aisle. "I have to tell you something important," I whispered as we went out. "I'm sorry."

"What is it?"

I told her what I'd heard.

"What do you think they're up to, Daniel?" she

asked. "Do they plan to do something bad?"

"I think they're trying to steal those white dolphins."

"How will they do that?"

"I don't know, but I want to follow that Gary when he comes out. Listen, Yo-Yo, go meet Mom and Dad and see if you can get the keys to the motor home. I need my blue bag. Make sure it has Jim's fins in it — and my face mask, okay?"

"Daniel, you're not going to try to get into the waterways, are you?"

"I hope I don't have to, " I said.

"Why don't I get Jim to help you?"

"He'll never believe me. Anyway, he may not be with Mom and Dad. Now hurry. Meet me down there, near those windows where people are waiting to see the white dolphins swim back through to their tanks."

"What if Dad won't let me go to the motor home alone?"

"Then let him go with you. Just tell him I wanted my bag! You don't have to say why I want it."

I waited with the people who couldn't get into the dolphin show. They were waiting for a glimpse of the creatures as they swam back through. I hoped the show wouldn't end before Yo-Yo got back. I began to worry that Dad would insist on knowing what I wanted, and why I hadn't stayed with her, and how I expected her to go out to the motor home by herself.

In about ten minutes, while there was still time before the end of the show, Yo-Yo came running back with Jim. "I had to tell him!" she said. "Dad sent him to meet us because Maryann and Mom and Dad are in line for the second dolphin show. They're saving a place for him!"

"What's this all about, Dan?" Jim said.

I told him the whole story, and I pleaded with him to believe that I hadn't made it up. "Doesn't it sound like they're going to try to kidnap the dolphins?" I asked.

"It sure does," he admitted. "I'm going to get one of those brochures that tells where all the underground waterways are. You take the keys to the motor home and get the gear — everything but the aqualung. I don't think I could sneak that past anybody."

I raced out to the gate, had my hand stamped by the ticket seller so I could get back in, and was soon picking through the back end of the motor home. I tried to put everything Jim wanted in one bag. It was hot and humid in the home, but I didn't mind. I just hoped we could keep that Gary from getting the white dolphins into his boat.

When I got back, Jim told me that a short man with dark hair and lots of hair on his arms and chest went into a door marked "Authorized Personnel Only." He said he was carrying an aqualung and a wet suit.

"That had to be him!" I said. "What are we going to do?"

"Keep watching through the windows," Jim said. "Watch for the white dolphins!" He ran off to the washroom and came back a few seconds later in his swim trunks. He was carrying his flippers, two masks, and the snorkel.

"Here they come!" Yolanda shouted. And people crowded around the windows in the steamy underground hallway to see the white dolphins glide by. As they moved out of sight, and everyone turned away, Jim and Yo-Yo and I kept our noses pressed up against the glass.

"That's him!" I said, as a black-suited diver kicked past, heading toward the dolphins. He touched them, and played with them, as if he knew what he was doing. They nipped at a bag tied around his waist which held what looked like salmon and other fish.

He pulled out a couple of fish and tossed them ahead of the dolphins. Anyone watching would have thought he was an authorized feeder or trainer. Jim ran down the hallway, leaving his gear on the floor next to me — masks, flippers, knife, everything.

I gathered it all up, including the brochure he'd been studying. Yolanda and I ran after him, but he was gone. We pressed up against the glass again, but all we could see were the tails of the white dolphins, moving quickly away from us.

9

Jim Disappears

I ran through the underground hallways, trying to find where Jim had gone, trying not to get too far ahead of my sister, trying to hang on to all Jim's gear, trying to keep track of the white dolphins, and wondering what I was supposed to do.

"Look at the paper!" Yo-Yo shouted behind me. It was a good idea. I was getting nowhere with all this running. Jim was long gone, and the white dolphins were out of sight. Also, I had lost track of the man in the black wet suit.

So I stopped and leaned up against the clammy wall. After I caught my breath, I looked at the brochure. People gave us dirty looks because we'd been running all around and shouting at each other, but I didn't care. I was afraid Jim was in trouble, and we had to help him.

Besides, no one should be allowed to kidnap dolphins, even if they *are* worth a lot of money.

The map of the underground waterways showed tunnels snaking out in many directions. I tried to follow the most likely route from the water show to the holding tanks. Then I tried to guess which way someone would try to lead the dolphins, when trying to take them to the southern inlet.

A young man walked by in an orange jacket. It had "Marineland" on the back. "Sir," I called, "can you tell me something?"

"I don't know," he said, turning around. "I'm new here."

"Oh, I was just wondering if the dolphins have to be led back to their tanks after the show."

"No, they don't. One of the first things they're trained to do is get back to their own tanks. There are clocks outside that tell the spectators when they'll be back, and they're usually right on time."

Yolanda and I ran to the tank of the white dolphins. A sign said they were supposed to be back at 2:30 and leave again at 3:00 for the next show. A crowd was still waiting for them. The tank was empty, but it was only 2:40.

"Have they already been here?" Yo-Yo asked.

"No," someone said. Some others shook their heads. "Maybe the show ran late, or they're going to stay out there for the next one."

We knew that couldn't be true. The white dolphins performed at the end of the show. They couldn't stay underwater that long. Anyway, we had seen them leave. Gary's plan was working. He had led the white dolphins away from their tank.

I looked at the map again. "Look, Yo-Yo," I said, pointing to the waterway that led to the left of the tanks — and south toward the inlet. "Isn't that the only place he could be leading them?"

She shrugged. "I don't know, Daniel. I guess so. Is that south?" I nodded. "Then that has to be it! But how do we stop them?"

I handed her the two face masks but kept the flippers and snorkel. We went running off again, looking for an entrance to the waterway that led to the inlet.

Our journey quickly took us past where most of the tourists were walking. I looked at the map again. The only way to follow the waterway we wanted was to run through a tunnel marked "Private! Do Not Enter!"

Instead of a locked door, there was just a chain draped across the entrance. I skidded to a stop in front of it. "This is probably where Jim went," I said. "Do you think we should—"

Before I could even finish my question, Yo-Yo had scooted under the chain and was running through the hallway. It was dark and dingy and scary. It smelled of muck and fish and chemicals, and it was lit only by little, yellow bulbs every ten feet or so.

Instead of big viewing windows like all the other tunnels had — so the people could watch the fish going back and forth — this long, steamy hallway had small, thin, dirty windows. We could just barely see the water channel running on the other side.

The only light was from the sky above the water. If there had been any big creatures swimming through, we would have seen them. None were being delivered from the inlet, and the ones we were chasing, we were sure, had already passed through.

I was worried about Jim. I stopped and knelt to study the wet tracks on the cold pavement between the drains. Someone had recently run through all right, and the feet looked large. If you could tell anything by looks, they looked like thong tracks.

"What was Jim wearing on his feet, Yo-Yo?" I asked.

"Thongs," she said. And we kept running.

Just when I thought I couldn't run any further, we came to a heavy door at the end of the tunnel. I opened it, and we charged up the stairs and burst into the brilliant sunshine. It took a minute to get used to the light, but the first thing I saw were Jim's thongs.

They had been kicked aside at the base of a high wire fence. There were footprints in the tall grass between the fence and the cement channel.

We ran along the outside of the fence for about a hundred yards, keeping our eyes on the tracks inside the fence next to the water. When the channel dipped underground to go through a cement tunnel, we saw that the flattened-out steps in the grass led down into the water.

"Yo-Yo!" I yelled, stopping and peering through the fence. "Jim went into the tunnel!"

"How could he breathe under there?"

"I don't know! I don't think he can!" The tunnel led another hundred yards or so to the inlet off the Atlantic. "See, it leads out to the boat."

"That must be the kidnappers' boat," she said.

I nodded, praying silently that Jim had not drowned in that tunnel. He must have been trying to follow Gary as he led the dolphins along. "Jim doesn't have *any* swimming gear!" I shouted. "Just his trunks!"

"Is he going to die under there?" Yolanda

I've got to help him.

asked, almost crying. "I couldn't stand that."

"Not if I can help it," I said. "Get ready to toss me the flippers and the masks."

I climbed the fence, but as I reached the top Yolanda was crying. "Daniel, you can't swim that far underwater! Do you want the snorkel? I'll throw it over!"

"The snorkel's no good underwater," I said. "Jim might be able to make it out to the inlet without air, but it will take him almost two minutes. He'll be short of breath from running, too."

I dropped to the ground. "Throw the stuff over!" I said.

"Daniel, you have to promise you're not going in there!"

"Yo-Yo! I have to!"

"Maybe he made it out already!"

"Maybe he didn't!"

"Well, at least run up to the other end and see! You won't be able to see him in the tunnel anyway! There's no light once you get away from the opening!"

I looked at the tunnel. She was right. If Jim was in there, I'd never be able to find him. The tunnel was wide and deep and completely underwater. There wasn't even an air pocket near the top where I could get a quick breath if I needed it. By now Jim had to have run out of his own air.

"I might be able to make it with the flippers," I said. "Throw them over."

"No, Daniel! I won't! And if you try to come and get them, I'll run away with them!"

"Yo-Yo!" I yelled. "I *have* to try to save Jim!"

"I'm not going to lose two brothers today!" she cried. "I just know Jim's already dead! I just know it!"

"All right," I said thinking quickly, "I'll look at the other end. I'll go in from that way. He had to make it more than halfway from there. Fair enough?"

"Okay!" she said, running south. I ran, too, on the inside of the fence near the underground tunnel. There the tall grass made it almost impossible to keep from slipping and falling.

About fifty feet offshore, the boat was working its way into position. I thought I saw one of the white dolphin's fins as it sliced through the water. "Is that one of them?" I shouted.

"Yes!" Yolanda yelled. "Do you see Jim?"

"No!" All I saw were air bubbles on the surface. They could have been from the dolphins' blowholes, or they could have been from Gary's aqualung. "I have to go into the tunnel!" I shouted. "Throw the stuff over!"

Yolanda slung the masks and the flippers over the fence as I tore off my clothes. I located where the underground tunnel came out into the water, put on the flippers and one mask, and held the other under my arm. I hoped Jim would be able to use it.

The pilot was backing the boat toward shore, not far from where Yolanda stood. "Get down behind the rock!" I said as loudly as I dared. "Don't let him see you!" I didn't know what he might do if he saw her.

She crouched low, hiding Jim's knife and snorkel. The pilot of the boat threw a rope over a metal pole on shore, then he went below deck. For a split second, I looked into Yolanda's eyes. We were both thinking the same thing.

I took a deep breath and flung myself into the water. As I worked my way down to the tunnel opening, I knew what Yo-Yo was doing. She was using Jim's super-sharp knife to cut that boat loose from the pole. It might not slow them down long, but it would help. There was nothing she could do for Jim. But if he was all right, she could stall the kidnappers long enough so that maybe we could stop them.

Just before pushing my way into the tunnel, I took one last look toward the boat. I could see both dolphins playfully diving around the scuba diver, nipping at the fish he kept tossing in front of them.

Yolanda had been successful. It had taken her several seconds, but I knew she had cut the rope. The boat began to rock and drift away from the shore. Gary had to forget the dolphins for a minute to signal the pilot that the boat was moving out of position. Gary waved frantically, and in a few seconds I felt the vibrations as Andy started the engine again.

With the first kick of my feet into the tunnel, I could see Jim struggling. His eyes were large, and his cheeks were puffed out as he tried to keep from taking in any water. He sure looked glad to see me!

I signaled that he was just a few feet from the end of the tunnel, and he gave one last surge. He could see the surface, and he went for it as fast as he could. As soon as his head was out of the water, he lay back and sucked air for all he was worth.

I was out of breath already, too, but all our activity had attracted one of the dolphins. We felt the movement of water beneath us as the bigger one, the male, glided under us toward the tunnel.

We knew Gary couldn't be far behind.

10

The Kidnapping

"I was close to them for a while," Jim said, between gasps for air. "I could feel the movement of the water in the tunnel, but I didn't know how long the tunnel was. After about a minute I thought about going back, but I knew he had to be taking them to the inlet, so I kept going."

I was proud that I'd helped him make it, but I didn't want to say anything about it. "Where's Yo-Yo?" he asked, suddenly realizing that she should be with me.

I pointed over to the rock where she had been hiding before she cut the rope with Jim's knife. But she wasn't there! "Oh, no," I said. Jim and I began to swim to shore to look for her, just as the male dolphin darted into the tunnel with Gary in pursuit.

"I don't think he's seen us yet," Jim said. "He's too worried about those dolphins."

Jim's knife was out of its sheath and lay by the rock near Yo-Yo's clothes. "Where's the snorkel?" I asked. Jim had a terrified look on his face as he pointed to the boat.

There, kicking and paddling on the surface, her face underneath and the snorkel sticking up, was Yolanda. She was checking out the kidnappers' boat. As Jim ran toward the water, I yelled, "Here!" and tossed him the flippers.

He hopped along, getting them on just before he dived in and rushed to Yo-Yo. He yanked her up and told her to follow him back. "Nobody's seen me yet, Jim!" she said. "I saw that you were okay — and I wanted to see if they caught the dolphins yet."

"They didn't!" he said. "Now come on! You're going to get yourself killed!"

"They did, too, Jim!" she said, scrambling up onto the beach. "The smaller dolphin is in a cage down there! That's why the guy didn't see me. He was too busy shutting the cage."

"We have to get back behind those rocks before he comes up to secure the boat again," Jim said. And we ran to hide. "After he secures it, we'll wait until he goes below. Then we'll cut the line again. That was good work, Yolanda."

Look! There she is.

She smiled, but I could tell she was just as scared as I was. "Will Gary be able to catch that other dolphin, Jim?" I asked.

"He'll probably lure him back with food. He wouldn't be able to catch a dolphin that didn't want to be caught, but these dolphins think they're being played with."

"Here comes the male and Gary!" I said, pointing to bubbles on the surface near the entrance to the tunnel.

"He won't be able to get him into the cage unless the boat is steady," Jim said.

"Duck!" I said. "Here comes Andy." The pilot hurried to the steering wheel and worked the boat around to the stake. Then he skipped down and threw the rope around it, and tied it again. He left the boat running, and he strapped on an aqualung before going below.

"The longer we keep them from knowing we're here, the better," Jim said. "We just have to keep bothering them, so they can't take the dolphins until the show officials realize they're gone."

"Then what?"

"Then they'll come looking for them, I hope," Jim said. "The dolphins should be heading for the show right now. When they don't turn up, there will be a lot of scared people looking for them. This is the only other place they could be."

The problem, however, was that the male dolphin and Gary were getting closer to the boat. When Jim was sure that he couldn't be seen, he whipped off the fins, grabbed the knife, and raced to the stake. He quickly sliced through the rope and hurried back to us.

The boat, its engine still idling, brushed up against the bank of the inlet and drifted away again. Something Gary did near the cage made the male dolphin leap from the water in a small arch and head for the open sea.

"We can't let that happen," Jim said, putting the fins on again. "I'm going to have to risk letting them see me." He took the knife and jumped into the water. I had no idea what he was going to do, but I knew he'd have trouble by himself with one free dolphin, one caged, and two kidnappers with oxygen tanks.

I jumped in behind Jim with the other face mask. The first thing we saw was Andy heading back up to secure the boat, and Gary taking off after the male dolphin. The female was caged just as Yo-Yo had said.

Jim turned to me and pointed to the other side of the boat. There we could come up for air without being seen by either Andy or Gary. Gary was flipping small fish out ahead of him as he swam after the dolphin. And it worked.

The big creature made a fast turn in the water and headed back toward the boat, just as we were going under it to come up on the other side. We still hadn't been seen. As we popped above the water, Jim said, "I hope Yo-Yo stays right where she is."

Neither of us could risk peeking around the end of the boat to make sure she was safe, so we went under. We watched as Gary and Andy tried to get the big dolphin into the cage along with the female.

The boat continued to drift, and as the female banged against the sides of the cage, she made the boat bounce and move farther from shore. Gary and Andy looked at each other as if they had figured something out.

Either someone was loosening that line every time, or Andy didn't know how to secure it. Gary signaled that he would go up. He gave some of the fish from his bag to Andy to keep the male dolphin close.

Jim pointed up with his thumb, and we surfaced just as Gary reached the deck of the boat. He slipped off his aqualung and set it in the bow with the remaining fish. As he moved to the other side of the craft to start the engine, and to get into position to secure the line again, he noticed Yolanda peeking around the big rock.

"Hey!" he yelled, leaving the wheel and rushing to the edge of the boat. "You been messing with this line?"

She turned and ran back toward the park. As Gary called after her, Jim reached over the side with his knife and cut the hose of Gary's aqualung. When he slipped back down to where I was, he also had the rest of Gary's fish.

Andy surfaced. "I'm losing him!" he said. "Come down and help!"

"All right," Gary said, quickly tying the line. "It was just a kid messing with the rope. A little girl. Hey, did you take the rest of my fish?" he asked as he strapped on his tank and sat on the edge of the boat. But Andy had already gone under.

Gary turned his oxygen on as he was falling backward into the water. The great rush of air was his first clue that his hose had been cut. He came straight back up, thrashing and gasping and coughing.

"Somebody's on the boat!" he screamed. "Somebody cut my hose!!" He leaped onto the boat and grabbed his compressed gas spear gun. Frantically he looked all through the boat for whoever had cut his hose.

Jim knew that when he found no one, he

would be back in the water and ready to shoot anything that moved. Anything, that is, except those expensive white dolphins.

Jim whispered a plan to me as fast as he could. "It'll be dangerous," he said, "but it's our only chance. Go down with this fish and get the dolphin to take it from you. Are you afraid of him?"

"The dolphin? No," I said, shaking my head, but I wasn't really that sure.

"As soon as he takes it, grab his back fin with your left hand and his tail fin with your right. I'll throw two or three fish as far as I can toward the tunnel opening. He'll go for 'em, so hang on. Get a good breath before you go down, because he'll probably take you all the way through the tunnel. As soon as you see daylight, let go. You will probably come up right about where I left my thongs. Ready?"

"Yeah, but what are you gonna be doing?"

"Trying to free that female. Don't worry about Andy. I don't think he's armed. But we have to stay away from Gary's spear gun."

11

The
Battle

Andy had used up the rest of his bait. So when I took my deep breath and went under, I found the big dolphin eager to accept what I had to offer.

I also found, of course, a very surprised and angry pilot who had expected to see his partner.

He waved at me and shook his head. Then he moved close and bumped me hard. I quickly held my last two fish in front of the dolphin.

Just as he snapped them from my hands, I grabbed hold of him as Jim had told me. Three fish plopped into the water near the entrance of the tunnel, almost fifty feet away.

I was off on a ride that no roller coaster could match. And was I scared! I tried to keep my eyes open as the big creature whipped his tail back and forth and shot over to the bait.

He caught the fish in his mouth as they fell. He spied the tunnel opening and kept going. I hoped I could hold my breath long enough to make it to the surface at the other end.

I closed my eyes. If I could just think about holding the air in, this big animal would escape the kidnappers. But suddenly he turned around!

It was as if he heard something I couldn't hear. Maybe it was something thrashing near the boat. Maybe it was the spear gun. Maybe it was the sound of fighting. Maybe it was special noises from the other dolphin. I didn't know.

All I knew was that we were more than halfway through the tunnel when he turned around. Should I let go and try to swim to the surface at the other end — or should I just hang on and go up when we came out near the boat?

While I was thinking about it, I hung on. The dolphin went faster on the way back, as if to help his mate. I opened my eyes, but the tunnel was pitch black. I had never wanted to see light more in my life.

I squinted and looked far ahead. My heart was pounding harder and harder, and faster and faster. I felt as if my lungs would burst. I kept telling myself not to panic.

But I knew I couldn't hold on much longer. I felt my strength leaving me. *Hold on,* I told myself, *hold on, hold on, hold on!* My left hand slipped off the back fin, but I was able to grab onto the tail fin with it.

Now I had two hands on the tail fin. My legs dangled straight back as he pulled me toward the end of the tunnel, and I nearly fainted for lack of air.

I had held my breath for so long that I knew some would have to come out. So I let a little out through my lips. All that did was make me want to let it all out and take a big, deep breath.

But that would kill me. I knew it. That would fill my lungs with water, and I would lose consciousness and drop to the bottom.

Just when I didn't think I could last another second, and just when my fingers slipped away from the slick tail fin, I saw the light of the sky near the surface.

As the dolphin headed straight for his mate in the cage, I used my last ounce of strength to kick and push. As I did, my head popped through to fresh air.

Everything ached — my head, my arms, my wrists, my hands, my fingers, my chest, my stomach. I panted and panted, but I knew I had to go back under to see what was happening with Jim.

As soon as I was able, I stuck my head below. I

saw Andy grabbing at Jim's flippers, as Jim tried to come up for air. Gary was trying to work his spear out of the side of the boat. Apparently he had shot and missed Jim by less than a foot.

I came back up, certain I hadn't been seen yet, and swam to the boat. I climbed up into the hull and jumped over to the other side, grabbing Jim's hand just as he came up.

With his other hand Jim tossed the knife into the boat. As his head bobbed up, he yelled, "Try to cut the cage away from the boat if you can!" And then he was pulled back under.

I wondered why he hadn't used his knife to keep Andy from grabbing his feet. But I knew Jim would never hurt anyone unless he had to.

I grabbed the knife and jumped back in the water, sliding down between the back of the boat and cage. I found myself next to the heavy rope that attached the cage to the boat. I saw the fearful look in the eyes of the female dolphin as she continued to thrash inside the cage.

The male dolphin was circling, obviously afraid, and not equipped to charge like a shark. Gary had dropped his aqualung to the bottom. He had moved next to Andy to share his air.

But Andy was so busy pulling on Jim's flippers that he ignored him. Gary had to rise to the surface to breathe.

Jim let both flippers slide from his feet into Andy's hands. Then he surfaced again for a gulp of air. I was sawing away at the rope, and doing fairly well, but I was soon weak again and short of breath.

Just as I decided to go up for some air, Gary came back down and spotted me for the first time. I kicked right up past him and hung on the side of the boat by my elbows while I gulped in more air.

When I went back down, Gary grabbed my left arm so tightly I thought he'd snap my wrist. Without thinking, I whirled to face him and thrust Jim's long, sharp blade to within four inches of his face.

His eyes grew large, but he didn't let go until I pushed the knife even closer to his eyes. When I was free, I pushed up with my arms and kicked at his face with my feet. He took in some water and went up for air.

I wanted to finish cutting the cage free from the boat, just in case these guys got the idea they could get away. But Andy had grabbed Jim's legs, wrapping his long arms around both knees.

Jim was helpless. He tried to swing at Andy, but, without the use of his legs, he had no balance in the water. I saw Jim come completely

He's trying to drown him!

under. While he was swinging with everything he had, Andy was just hanging on and pulling him down.

I'll never forget the look of terror in Jim's eyes as he realized that he was in the death grip of someone who had a lot of air left in his tank. Jim stared over at me, and I knew I had to do something.

I put my feet up against the side of the boat and pushed off. The push sent me around the cage and almost into Andy's tanks. I reached out with the knife and sliced right through both air hoses. Suddenly Andy was busy with both arms and legs, trying to get to the surface.

Jim grabbed the other side of the boat, and I followed him up. Gary was trying to loosen the rope for the getaway. As the other three of us gasped for air, we all finally got a good look at each other.

I was the only one with a weapon now, but Gary ran and got another spear gun. He whirled toward us, and we ducked. But the loud pop was close enough to hurt my ears.

The three-pronged spearhead pierced Andy's shoulder and sent him tumbling back, his blood clouding the water. Gary ran over to help him into the boat. "Let's go!" he said. "The male will follow us because we have the female. They stick together! Where one goes, the other one goes also."

"Give me the knife, Dan!" Jim yelled, as Gary maneuvered the boat away from the bank of the inlet.

I handed it to him and went down to help. The male dolphin was staying close. As Gary moved the craft out into the ocean, Jim and I were hanging onto the cage and working together to cut it free.

12

The Rescue

The water rushing from the back of the speeding boat, and the energy it took just to hang on, made it hard for us to stay underwater very long. When we surfaced for air, Andy was piloting the boat, and Gary was reloading his gun.

"Just hold the rope tight so I can cut it!" Jim yelled as he went down again, gripping the side of the cage. I wedged myself between the back of the boat and the top of the cage. I spread out as far as I could so the rope would be tight.

Within seconds, Jim had cut through the rope and the cage slowly dropped about twenty feet to the bottom. We rode it all the way down. Jim pointed to where the boat was and then down. I nodded as we surfaced. Another few feet out

They saved the dolphin!

and the cage would have dropped to about forty feet.

The male dolphin was still close by. "Gary was right," Jim said, taking off his mask and treading water. "The dolphins are gregarious," he added, panting. "That means they like each other's company. The male would have followed that cage, and he'll stay with it."

"Should we open it so they can go back to the park?" I asked.

"I wouldn't risk it," Jim said. "They might be frightened enough to head for the open sea. Anyway, look," he added, pointing to the shore where Yolanda was waving with both arms.

The shore was covered with security vehicles, squad cars with lights flashing, two small motorboats being launched, and a lot of official-looking people. "You see Mom and Dad?" I asked.

"No," Jim said, sounding suddenly very tired. "But I'm sure they're up there."

"Jim," I said, overcome with what we had been through, "I don't know if I can swim back." I began to panic. "In fact, I don't think I can stay above water much longer."

"I know how you feel," he said. "Hang on, they're coming to get us."

"I mean it, Jim!" I said. "I'm weak."

"Okay, partner," he said, not sounding so strong himself. He moved close and told me to wrap my arms around his neck from behind.

"You sure you can hold me?" I asked, not knowing what I would do if he said no.

"Course," he said, "I can do anything, remember?" He laughed. I tried to, but I was nearly asleep. I floated in the water, resting my head against the back of his, and putting my weight on his shoulders. The muscles across his back felt hard and tight.

I wanted to cry, but not in front of Jim. I knew I would later. I was still remembering my scary ride through the tunnel, and that Gary guy grabbing me underwater. I could have drowned many times.

The motorboats cut their engines when they were a little way off. "You guys all right?" a security guard called out. Then I saw Dad in the back of the other boat, ready to help us in.

"We need a lift," Jim said. "Start with the little guy here. The dolphins are right below us."

"You're kidding! You kept them from taking the dolphins?"

Jim nodded. "The female's in a cage, and the male is right next to her." A diver jumped over the side with a line, and, while one boat took us back to shore, the other towed the cage — with the male following — to the mouth of the tunnel. There divers led the dolphins back into the park.

Yolanda had run back for help when Gary spotted her. By the time she found Mom and Dad and Maryann, the park officials already knew something was wrong.

The trainer of the dolphin show was concerned when the male didn't appear at his scheduled time for the second show. And, when neither white dolphin appeared several minutes later, he took a break in the show and asked his aides to locate them.

They weren't in their tank, of course, so divers were sent through the waterways. They had just started toward the inlet when Dad and Mom and Yolanda and Maryann reached the security office.

Yolanda had described the boat and Gary, and the Coast Guard cut them off before they were far from the inlet. Once Gary and Andy realized that the cage had been cut loose, they just thought about escaping. But they didn't get far.

During their questioning, they told the police about Jonas, the older man I had seen at the dolphin show. A few other people were arrested, too, including one man who had worked with Gary at the marine park.

Our whole family talked in Mom and Dad's hotel room until late that night about the adventure. I knew none of my friends would believe it, unless I showed them the newspaper from the next day's paper.

The headline on the front page read: *Prep Basketball Star, Brother Foil Marine Kidnap.*

Jim and I agreed that the story didn't give Yo-Yo enough credit. But she didn't mind. She said she was so scared that we were going to drown all she wanted was to see us alive again.

Of course, that day in St. Augustine was the most exciting of my life, and I'll never forget it —even though there are parts of it I don't like to think about.

But, you know? That morning with Jim on the beach was just as important to me as the afternoon with him and the dolphins and the kidnappers.

He says I saved his life a couple of times, and maybe I did. But I can never thank him enough for what he did for me at dawn.

A brand new series!

The Jennifer Books

By Jane Sorensen

Jennifer Green talks to God. Everyday. Often, several times a day. In her first book, **It's Me, Jennifer,** she's twelve years old when she meets God by going to Sunday school for the first time. There she learns that God is her friend and she begins to tell Him about the important things in her life. Things like her first high-school basketball game, her first two-piece swimsuit, her first game of tennis with a boy (was that a *date*, Lord?), and her exciting, but disappointing Christmas.

Just before the end of seventh grade, she finds out that **It's Your Move, Jennifer,** because her dad has been promoted and the whole family will be moving to Philadelphia. What's it like to leave the only home, school, and friends you've ever known? Find out as Jennifer does and as she shares her thoughts with God.

In **Jennifer's New Life,** Jennifer adjusts to a new city, new school, new friends, and her first church retreat. The speakers at the retreat help her to understand that God wants to be more than just her friend, and she becomes a Christian. Now she faces a new set of problems: What will the kids at school think? What will her parents and younger brothers think? The retreat leader said she would share Christ with at least one other person – how can she do *that?* Together with God, Jennifer finds the answers.

Finally, in **Jennifer Says Good-bye,** Jennifer experiences some very grown-up emotions. She begins to understand how deeply she can love another family member, and how very much it hurts when that person dies. But through the sorrow that she shares with her family, something wonderful begins to happen and Jennifer learns that kids can be a great help to their parents.

If you *ever* have to deal with emotions like fear, loneliness, excitement, wanting to belong, disappointment, learning to love, or sorrow, you'll enjoy reading **The Jennifer Books.**

How lucky can some kids get?

It seems like Eric and Alison, the Thorne twins, are always running into adventure. The most ordinary things become unusual when they are involved.

The Great UFO Chase   In this seventeenth book of the series, a brainy student visits the Thornes, and brings with him a lot more than his books! Is it purely coincidental that residents of Ivy, Illinois, begin sighting UFO's just after this stranger arrives? What kind of transmission is disturbing the radio-station signals, and why are Air Force officials interested in the Thornes' houseguest? Eric asks these questions and more before he finally finds the answers to *The Great UFO Chase*.

The Olympic Plot   Alison unknowingly becomes a threat to the lives of the President and Vice President of the United States. She knows only that she is not in complete control of her actions, and that she forgets segments of time. How can she help Eric uncover the plot when neither of them is sure there *is* a plot? Their visit to Olympic Village becomes a nightmare of kidnappings, fake athletes, and sickness, while the time for murder draws closer and closer.

Secret of Pirates' Cave   When a classmate of Eric's presents an exciting report of how pirates once raided his ancestors, Eric repeats the story at home. He and Alison are thrilled to discover that their own ancestors were on the same ship, and were raided by the same pirate. Mr. Thorne shows them half of a map that supposedly leads to the families' treasure, and the search is on!

Before the treasure can be recovered, the kids must deal with secret tunnels, a "monster cave," and a ghost who doesn't want the past disturbed!

If you like adventure stories, be sure to read these and other books in the Thorne Twin series.

Brand-new series!

The Bradford Family Adventures

Daniel's Big Surprise   Daniel Bradford is eleven years old, and the youngest member of his family. He sometimes feels confused and sometimes gets angry with his family, but Daniel's biggest problem is loneliness. This book is about what happens when he goes looking for a friend. He finds more than one friend, takes some big steps towards growing up, and, in the end, gets a wonderful surprise!

Two Runaways   This book is about lies. What happens when kids lie, when adults do or do not believe them, when a kid's reputation for honesty is destroyed? This book is also about bravery, courage, and forgiveness. If you've ever told a lie—or had one told about you—you'll understand Daniel's problem. And maybe you'll know a little more about what to do the next time you are tempted to lie.

The Clubhouse Mystery   Yolanda Bradford is only nine when she discovers how tricky temptation can be. When her own curiosity gets her into serious trouble, Yolanda has to try hard to do what's right. It takes a lot of courage, but with her big brothers' and sister's help, she manages.
   From this tense situation, Yolanda learns that it is easier to *stay* out of trouble than to *get* out, and she later proves that she remembers the lesson.

The Kidnapping   Daniel and Yolanda are too young to tangle with kidnappers, even with their big brother Jim's help. The adventure is very exciting and Daniel learns just how brave he can be, but that is not the most important thing he learns. When Daniel and Jim spend some private time together, they talk about God, and what it means to worship Him. You'll want to read about Daniel's feelings and the wonderful experience he shares with Jim.